J COR
Broken arrow

INVISIBLE SIX 6

BROKEN ARROW

BY: JIM CORRIGAN
ILLUSTRATED BY: KEV HOPGOOD

Claw
An Imprint of Magic Wagon
abdobooks.com

For Sgt. 1st Class Javier J. Gutierrez and Sgt. 1st Class Antonio R. Rodriguez of the 7th Special Forces Group (Airborne), who died in a firefight in Nangarhar Province, Afghanistan, on Feb. 8, 2020. —JC

For my invisible backup team, Louis, Rory, Evie, and Heather. Without them, no mission gets off the ground. —KH

abdobooks.com

Printed in the United States of America, North Mankato, Minnesota.
052021
092021

 THIS BOOK CONTAINS RECYCLED MATERIALS

Written by Jim Corrigan
Illustrated by Kev Hopgood
Edited by Meg Gaertner
Art Direction by Jake Slavik

Library of Congress Control Number: 2020948610

Publisher's Cataloging-in-Publication Data

Names: Corrigan, Jim, author. | Hopgood, Kev, illustrator.
Title: Broken arrow / by Jim Corrigan ; illustrated by Kev Hopgood.
Description: Minneapolis, Minnesota : Magic Wagon, 2022. | Series: Invisible Six
Summary: A cargo plane carrying nuclear weapons vanishes in a cyclone. Bicep and Invisible Six must recover the missiles before they fall into the wrong hands.
Identifiers: ISBN 9781098230432 (lib. bdg.) | ISBN 9781644945742 (pbk.) | ISBN 9781098230999 (ebook) | ISBN 9781098231279 (Read-to-Me ebook)
Subjects: LCSH: Special forces (Military science)--Juvenile fiction. | Special operations (Military science)--Juvenile fiction. | Spy stories--Juvenile fiction. | Transport planes--Juvenile fiction. | Weapons of mass destruction--Juvenile fiction. | Terrorists--Juvenile fiction.
Classification: DDC [FIC]--dc23

TABLE OF CONTENTS

Athena

Role: Team Leader
Service History: Operations staff, 75th Ranger Regiment. Squadron commander, Delta Force.
Profile: Excels at tactics and strategy. Handles herself well in a firefight, but her time is best spent planning and maintaining situational awareness.

Shade

Role: Executive Officer
Service History: CIA Special Operations Group.
Profile: Recruited by the CIA right out of high school. Extensively trained in spy craft and covert ops. Businesslike and loyal.

Doc Dee

Role: Medic
Service History: Medical Department, USS *America* amphibious assault ship.
Profile: Believes in the unit's purpose but gives priority to his doctor's oath. Interested in all the arts and sciences, enabling him to offer out-of-the-box solutions.

Gizmo

Role: Tech Specialist
Service History: National Security Agency.
Profile: Recruited by software companies and the NSA after getting caught writing illegal modifications for video games. Solves problems in eavesdropping, countersurveillance, and codebreaking.

Zumi

Role: Jumpmaster/Rescuer/Mechanic
Service History: Puerto Rico Air National Guard, US Air Force Special Operations Command.
Profile: Joined the Air Guard to work on heavy equipment and parachute jump. Graduate and instructor of the Air Force pararescue school.

Bicep

Role: Infantryman
Service History: US Naval Special Warfare Command.
Profile: Accepted into Navy SEAL training, but dropped out for family reasons. Later returned to the Navy and joined Special Warfare Group 4. Serves as the team's parachute rigger and maritime expert.

TOP SECRET
(YOUR EYES ONLY)

From:
General Ledlie, Pentagon
To:
Special Operative BICEP
Mission Codename:
BROKEN ARROW

An unprecedented storm is sweeping the Pacific. We have lost contact with numerous bases and outposts. A US Air Force cargo jet has gone missing and is presumed lost at sea. Worse, I have just learned that the jet was carrying twenty tactical nuclear missiles. I need Invisible Six to recover these powerful weapons before they fall into the wrong hands.

OBJECTIVES:

- Proceed through the storm to Naval Station Pearl Harbor.

- Secure a vessel and outfit it with search equipment.

- Locate the crash site and dive to recover the nuclear missiles.

A C-17 Globemaster cargo jet staggered like a paper airplane through a darkening sky. High winds buffeted the jet. Sheets of rain pounded the cockpit windows.

The US Air Force plane was on a special mission. The C-17 carried twenty tactical nuclear missiles. The weapons were on their way to San Diego, California, to be decommissioned.

Extreme security measures had been put in place. Terrorists and rogue nations would do anything to possess nuclear weapons. So, the C-17 used aerial refueling. By meeting with tanker planes, it could stay airborne for the entire journey. But the unexpected storm was complicating things. It had kept the second fuel-laden tanker plane from making its rendezvous with the jet.

The jet's pilots knew they were in trouble. Their thirsty aircraft was skirting the edge of an unpredictable megastorm. Their calls for help went unanswered. They suspected the storm had knocked out communications. The dire lack of fuel meant they could not even turn back.

The pilots searched for an option—any option—to keep their plane from crashing into the sea.

The aircraft commander carefully studied the navigation display. She pointed to a speck of an island. "What about there?"

Her copilot shook his head. "I don't think we'd make it."

"We're out of choices," the commander said grimly. "If we're going to ditch in the water, I'd rather do it near an island."

"Adjusting course now," said the copilot.

The C-17 banked into the storm. Slate-gray clouds turned black. The pilots struggled with the flight controls as the airplane shuddered. A lightning bolt streaked so near they could hear its electric sizzle.

The fuel display flashed red.

"Mayday, Mayday," the commander spoke into the radio. "To anyone who might be receiving this message, this is a USAF C-17 jet flying under the call

sign Chalk One. We are declaring an emergency."

Four huge turbofan engines propelled Chalk One deeper into the storm. Their steady growl reassured the pilots. But as the plane's fuel tanks ran dry, the growl softened to a purr. One engine flamed out, and then another.

"We're at half power," the copilot warned. "Running on vapors."

The storm pushed them toward the ocean. Another engine went silent. The pilots fought for altitude, but it was no use.

The commander decided to send one last radio call. Nobody would hear it, she knew, but that didn't matter. It was proper procedure.

"This is Chalk One," she said into the static. "We're going down."

CHAPTER 1

HURRICANE HUNTERS

Naval Air Station North Island
San Diego, California
0645 Local / 6 NOV

Bicep stopped the Humvee and surveyed the station. It had gone into full lockdown because of the storm. Ground crews towed fighter jets and helicopters into hangars. Anchors held large transport planes snug against the concrete.

Bicep rubbed his shoulder, which seemed to ache only in times of stress. Typhoon Kilo, now twice the size of Texas, was churning across the Pacific like an angry sea monster. Meteorologists were already calling Kilo the worst storm in history.

Right now, Bicep's teammates were converging on San Diego from posts around the world. The loss of nuclear weapons, an example of what the military called a Broken Arrow incident, required urgent action. Bicep was the vanguard for this mission. He needed to have transportation to Hawaii ready when his teammates arrived. But with no aircraft flying, he was off to a rocky start.

The soft drone of distant propellers caught his attention. He turned and scanned the horizon. A C-130 Hercules cargo plane was approaching.

Bicep called to a nearby worker. "What's the story with that Herc?"

The sailor grabbed a pad and scrolled the flight log. "Sir, that's a hurricane hunter. It's stopping here for fuel before heading into the storm."

Most aircrews steered clear of hurricanes and typhoons. But the men and women of the 53rd Weather Reconnaissance Squadron intentionally flew into them. The squadron's WC-130J Weatherbirds were specially equipped for the job. Hurricane hunters gathered valuable data, helping scientists better understand violent storms.

"Where will it land after passing through the typhoon?" Bicep asked.

"Honolulu," the sailor said.

Bicep grinned broadly. "Is that so?"

Hours later, the Weatherbird rumbled down the runway and climbed aloft with I-6 on board. As the newly reunited I-6 teammates chatted and exchanged jokes, Bicep turned to the serious work ahead.

He found a quiet niche in the back of the plane and called up the map provided by General Ledlie. The search area, based on Chalk One's last known position, covered thousands of square kilometers.

"Bruh." Gizmo poked his head into the niche. "We're approaching the typhoon. Come check it out."

Bicep rubbed his shoulder. "No, thanks. I've got work to do."

Gizmo gave him a sideways glance. "You don't want to see?"

"I won't need to see it. I'll feel it." At Gizmo's insistent stare, Bicep sighed and showed him the map. "This search grid is the size of Wyoming. I have no idea how to find Chalk One."

"Don't sweat it," Gizmo said. "We'll work on it as a team."

"But I'm the lead," Bicep said.

"Look, the general chose you for your naval expertise. He doesn't expect you to do everything."

"I just don't want to let anyone down."

"Trust me, I know the feeling," Gizmo said. "Just do your best, and the rest will fall into place. Now, come check out the light show."

The rest of I-6 was already buckled in at the front of the plane. The hurricane hunters sat at their workstations, calling out sensor readings. The Weatherbird shivered and swayed as its reinforced airframe absorbed Kilo's punishment.

Gravity pressed on Bicep's chest as the plane began a sharp turn. It was like riding the world's largest roller coaster. A monitor showed the plane's position inside the swirling storm. The pilots were circling Kilo's eye, preparing to enter.

Bursting through the eyewall, the plane leveled off inside Kilo's bright, calm center. Bicep laughed, surprised by the remarkable transition. The Weatherbird corkscrewed upward as the crew collected some final readings.

"That's enough fun for now," called the pilot. "Let's get our passengers where they need to go."

After landing at Hickam Air Force Base, the hurricane hunters bid I-6 farewell, then taxied off to the fuel depot. They were anxious to get back inside the storm.

I-6 grabbed some chow. Afterward, Athena and Bicep rode over to US Pacific Fleet headquarters for a meeting with an admiral who had been briefed on the top-secret mission. An aide showed them into an office overlooking Pearl Harbor.

"The loss of Chalk One's aircrew

saddens me," said the admiral, shaking his head. "But the fact that we have missing nukes out there terrifies me."

"Sir, my team won't rest until we've recovered the missiles," pledged Athena.

"You'll get the resources you need. Just say the word, and I'll make it happen."

"Thank you, sir," Athena said. "Our top priority is a search vessel."

"What did you have in mind?"

Bicep leaned forward in his chair. "We need a fast, nimble craft with enough room to bring home the missiles. I believe an LCAC would be the perfect choice."

The admiral arched an eyebrow. "The Landing Craft, Air Cushion is no search vessel. LCAC is a hovercraft, designed to carry marines onto a beach."

"Admiral, an LCAC can reach nearly eighty kilometers per hour while loaded with tanks, troops, and trucks. It's even quicker when empty. It's the fastest way to cover the search grid."

"What about fuel?" the admiral said. "Your search may last for several days."

Bicep nodded. "We can put a large-capacity fuel bladder in the cargo area and still have room for the missiles."

The admiral sat back. "I do like creative thinking. But I must warn you—the LCAC offers little comfort. You're in for a loud, bumpy ride and lots of sea spray."

"No worries, sir," Athena said, smiling. "We've endured worse."

CHAPTER 2

FLOATING ON AIR

Naval Station Pearl Harbor
Pearl Harbor, Hawaii
0630 Local / 7 NOV

Dawn broke over the Pacific as I-6 prepared to depart. The admiral kept his word, delivering an LCAC stocked with fuel, rations, deep-sea recovery tools, and an inflatable tent for sleeping.

Zumi joined Bicep in the vessel's cockpit. They pulled on their headsets and radioed the harbormaster that they were getting underway. Bicep fired up the four turbine engines. Enormous fan blades began spinning. A cushion of air filled the LCAC's rubberized canvas skirt, lifting the deck above the water's surface.

Bicep placed his hands on the control yoke and his feet on the rudder pedals. He guided the LCAC away from the dock.

Zumi whistled. "Impressive. How much training have you had?"

"Six weeks."

"Is it more like steering a boat or flying a helicopter?" she asked.

"A little bit of both. Did you ever play air hockey?" At Zumi's nod, Bicep said, "Think of the harbor as an air hockey table and the LCAC as the puck. Right now, we're hovering just above the water's surface, which makes us very agile. Watch this."

Bicep put the vessel into a gentle spin. Zumi grinned as they twirled three hundred sixty degrees. Sea spray from the gigantic fans coated the windshield, so Bicep turned on the wipers. He nudged the LCAC forward, and they glided through the harbor. Zumi watched intently as he operated the controls.

"Let me try," she urged.

They switched seats. Within a few minutes, Zumi was getting the hang of it. Bicep shook his head in amusement. Zumi had a natural touch with machines.

Soon they passed the USS *Arizona* Memorial, a shrine straddling the sunken hull of the battleship. *Arizona* had gone down in 1941, after a Japanese bomb struck its forward ammo magazines. The explosion had torn the ship in half, killing more than one thousand crewmembers. Bicep's teammates stood at the rails and saluted *Arizona*, in keeping with tradition.

"As a kid, I must've read a hundred books about Pearl Harbor," Bicep said.

"Why were you so into it?" Zumi asked.

"The idea of a surprise attack intrigued me. I liked to pretend I was there, making a difference. Kind of weird, huh?"

"Kids called me weird for taking apart my dirt bike," Zumi said. "Weird is good."

They left the harbor and headed into open water. Bicep took the controls, pushing the hovercraft to full throttle.

"What's the plan once we reach the search area?" Zumi asked.

"We'll crisscross the grid, hoping to pick up Chalk One's emergency radio beacon."

Zumi frowned. "Wouldn't a satellite have picked up any signal by now?"

"Normally, yes," Bicep said. "A floating beacon sends out a signal strong enough for satellite detection. But it may have sunk in the storm."

"So we need to hope its signal reaches the water's surface."

"We'll be towing a sonar array," Bicep said. "The array cable stretches two kilometers behind us, away from the engine noise."

"Sounds like you've covered all the bases."

"I had plenty of help," Bicep said. "It was a team effort."

The morning sun climbed into a clear sky as the LCAC sped across a gentle swell. The monster storm was gone from this location.

Now it was time to pick up the pieces.

But three days later, the team still had not spotted an oil slick or floating wreckage. Their sensitive listening gear had heard no beacon. Chalk One, it seemed, had vanished without a trace.

Bicep stood at the rail with a pair of binoculars. He had just finished a twelve-hour shift at the helm. His eyes burned from fatigue and his shoulder ached, but still he felt driven to look.

Shade joined him. "Any luck?"

Bicep shook his head, yawning.

"You need some rack time, my friend," Shade said.

"I know. In a few minutes."

Together, they looked out on the featureless blue expanse. Early one morning, Bicep had glimpsed the gigantic flukes of a whale. It had been the only excitement in three days of searching.

"We just heard from the admiral," Shade said. "He ordered us to proceed to Wake Island, ninety kilometers from here."

Bicep frowned. "Why?"

"Wake Island Airfield has been radio

silent ever since the storm. He wants us to check it out."

"Can't he send someone else?" Bicep asked. "We're kind of in the middle of something."

"We're closest, and we could use a resupply," Shade said. "We'll spend the night at Wake and get a fresh start in the morning. Now, go get that rack time."

Bicep handed over the binoculars and rubbed his eyes. He went into the inflatable tent and crashed on one of the cots. The steady drone of fan blades lulled him to sleep.

When Bicep awoke, the hovercraft was quiet and still. He unzipped the tent flap. Stars twinkled above palm tree silhouettes. A beach glowed in the moonlight.

He found a trail of footprints on

the white sand. A flattened sign read: *Wake Island Airfield—Where America's Day REALLY Begins*. He tramped inland, irritated the team had left him behind.

Bicep passed through the twisted main gate. Kilo had ravaged this tiny base. A fallen communications tower had crushed the guard shack. Everywhere, the lights were out. Debris littered the streets.

"Hello?" he called. "Anyone here?"

When nobody answered, he drew his sidearm. A steady, mechanical thrum sounded like a gas-operated generator. He spotted the building it powered and crept for the door.

Bicep heard people laughing. Club music blared. For some reason, the base was hosting a party. He holstered his weapon and pulled back the door. Colorful, pulsing lights washed over him.

"Look who's finally awake!" someone shouted over the music. His teammates sat at a table just inside the door.

"What's going on?" Bicep grumbled. "Why did you let me sleep?"

"Blame me for that," said Doc Dee. "I told them you could use the rest."

"Why is there a party? We should be getting ready to shove off in the morning."

Everyone burst out laughing. They dragged him outside to the debris-strewn runway. In the moonlight, Bicep saw the hulking outline of a cargo plane.

"Chalk One?" he stammered.

Gizmo punched him on the arm. "We found it after all."

"The pilots were preparing to ditch in the water," Athena said. "Suddenly, as they descended through a cloud layer, there was the island right in front of them."

Bicep walked to the C-17. The battered plane rested on its belly, the result of crushed wheel struts. Deep gouges streaked the lower fuselage. A wing had been sheared away during the landing.

"Quite a feat of flying," Zumi said. "They'll probably get air medals."

"What about the missiles?" Bicep asked.

"Undamaged," Shade said. "Still in the cargo bay."

Bicep shook his head in disbelief. "Now I see the reason for a party."

"That's not all, bruh," Gizmo said. "We'll stay a few days to help get the base up and running. I bet we can squeeze in some beach time."

Bicep grinned. "Guess I need to sleep through the mission more often."

The outpost slowly returned to working status. Bicep and Zumi helped restore power, while Gizmo worked with a tech team on the communications network. Doc Dee aided the medical staff. More work remained, but the mood around the base was upbeat.

Typhoon Kilo had finally withered and died, but its aftermath lingered. Millions of people needed food, shelter, and drinking water. The US military, along with forces from other nations, embarked on a massive rescue mission. The joint operation would save countless lives.

Bicep readied the hovercraft for a return to Pearl Harbor. Normally, the team would catch a flight back, but Wake Island's runway remained closed. Nuclear weapons specialists needed to remove Chalk One's missiles. Only then could its shattered airframe be safely hauled away.

Meanwhile, the I-6 team fell into the habit of an early-morning run. Wake Island offered spectacular views of nature, making workouts a pleasure. On their third morning there, the teammates were jogging along a sandy path when movement on the horizon caught Bicep's eye. A cluster of black dots grew larger. Soon, he heard the familiar beat of helicopter blades.

"Is there a carrier or assault ship in the area?" he asked, pointing toward the sea.

"Negative," Athena said. "They're all taking part in the humanitarian mission."

"Then who are these guys?"

Shade squinted. "The only islands within chopper range belong to Tangonesia."

"Maybe they're coming to check on us," Doc Dee suggested.

"The Tang government isn't that friendly," Athena said. "I think we'd better get back to base."

They ran at double time as a dozen helicopters thundered overhead. Most were troop transports, but Bicep also saw two Mi-25D Hind armored gunships. They bore the Tang flag—a red triangle with crossed swords on a navy background.

I-6 reached the airfield perimeter. They

crouched behind scrub brush as a single helicopter set down. Captain Molina, Wake Island's base commander, marched out to meet it. Armed guards followed.

A Tang general stepped from the helicopter, surrounded by commandos. Opposing soldiers eyed one another warily as their officers spoke.

Choppers buzzed above the meeting like angry wasps. Bicep couldn't hear what was being said, but he could guess at what was happening. The Tang general, now visibly agitated, spoke with sneers and finger jabs. Captain Molina remained calm, but his tight jaw hinted at growing frustration.

"How many troops are in those helicopters?" asked Doc Dee.

Bicep did some quick math. "Probably around a hundred."

"And how big is Wake Island's garrison?"

"Ninety-five officers and enlisted personnel," Shade said. "Plus our team."

"It'd be a pretty even match if we didn't have to deal with those two Hinds," Zumi said. "They bring a ton of firepower."

Bicep agreed with her assessment. The armored gunships bristled with guns and rockets. They could shred the base in minutes.

"I don't get it," Gizmo said. "Why would Tangonesia suddenly have a problem with a small American base? The airfield has been here since the 1930s."

"Tangonesia is a nation of islands," Athena said. "The current regime claims Wake Island as part of its archipelago. The United Nations disagrees."

"Kilo gave the Tang government a

perfect opportunity," Shade added. "They saw a storm-damaged base cut off from protection because of the humanitarian effort. The closest carrier strike group is three or four days away."

The Tang general began shouting. Soldiers on both sides pointed their weapons. The Hind helicopters zoomed in closer, their nose-mounted autocannons trained on the Americans. Captain Molina stood with his fists on his hips.

Bicep's breathing quickened. His heart thumped wildly. He needed a weapon.

"Steady, people," Athena said calmly. "We'll get our chance."

The Tang general stared in silence for a moment, then threw his arms up and stormed to the helicopter. The commandos backed away with rifles raised. They, too, boarded the chopper, which lifted off and joined the swirling formation.

The Hinds hovered, capable of destroying the airfield. Captain Molina and his guards stood their ground. Then, just as it seemed the gunships would open fire, they reared up and led the transport choppers away. The thump of their blades faded in the distance.

Bicep exhaled. "Not the outcome I was expecting."

"Same here, bruh," Gizmo said.

"I think we just saw a show of force," Shade said. "The Tang general was hoping for a quick surrender, which would let him take the airfield without damaging it. His threats didn't work. Now he'll likely try a different tactic."

"Gear up and prepare to dig in," Athena ordered. "We can't permit Tang forces to seize this island, especially with Chalk One's nuclear missiles still stranded here."

"Do you think they know about the missiles?" Bicep asked.

"Doubtful," Athena said. "I believe their target is the long-coveted airfield. The missiles would be a bonus, one which we cannot let them have."

She and Shade hurried off to confer with Captain Molina. The rest of the team jogged down to the beach, anxious to retrieve their weapons from the hovercraft. But upon reaching the shore, they halted and stared at the horizon.

A huge armada steamed toward the island. Bicep spotted destroyers, cruisers, and cargo ships.

It was an invasion fleet.

CHAPTER 4

BEACH BATTLE

Southern Tip of Wake Island
Pacific Ocean
1430 Local / 13 NOV

The good news was that a US carrier strike group had been diverted to Wake Island. But it would never arrive in time to prevent the invasion. With a top speed of less than sixty-five kilometers per hour, the powerful armada was still several days away. Until then, I-6 and the airfield's garrison were on their own.

But the Tang invaders had made an error. Their ships should have slipped into position at night. By approaching in broad daylight, they'd given the island's defenders several hours to prepare. Captain Molina had asked I-6 to organize the defense. He wanted to take full advantage of the team's expertise.

Athena set up a command post in the airfield's control tower and doled out responsibilities. She assigned Bicep twenty troops and ten machine guns to defend the southern beach.

"It's a paltry force for such a big job," Athena admitted. "But it's all I can spare."

"We'll give them a warm welcome," Bicep promised. He led his troops down to the tree line and showed them where to place foxholes. These small pits would allow the soldiers to take cover from enemy fire. As the soldiers dug, Bicep moved the hovercraft to the safety of the lagoon. The LCAC was a high-value asset.

In a worst-case scenario, I-6 could use it to evacuate the island.

Back at the beach, Bicep considered his strategy. Wake Island's southern beach was a slender triangle that jutted into the sea like a fang. It would be tough to defend. Tang landing craft could approach it from two directions at once.

So, Bicep divided the beach into ten sectors and assigned each sector to a two-person fire team.

As the teams camouflaged their machine-gun nests, Bicep reassured them. "You only need to worry about your own sector, because your neighbors will be covering theirs. We'll get through this by sticking together."

He raised his binoculars and watched Tang cruisers and destroyers draw closer. "They're going to prep the beach soon.

Just stay down in your holes until the fireworks are over."

Naval bombardment was the classic beginning to a beach landing. Exploding shells softened up defenses and created instant foxholes for soldiers coming ashore. The shelling also gave a morale boost to nervous troops packed aboard landing craft.

Soon, the Tang warships opened fire. Their first few rounds fell short, hammering the waves. Then the gunners corrected their aim and moved the bombardment onto the beach. Plumes of sand left smoldering craters.

In his foxhole, Bicep covered his ears as exploding shells marched to the tree line. Shrapnel whistled overhead, showering him with leaf flecks. The damp little foxhole became Bicep's sanctuary,

sheltering him from the firestorm. The pit did not give complete security. But in this moment, it felt as safe as home.

Kaboom!

The nearby blast made Bicep's ears ring. Another thud followed, but this one was softer. Something poked his back. He opened his eyes to see palm fronds surrounding him. He looked behind him. A fallen palm tree covered his foxhole.

The barrage moved farther inland. Bicep pushed his way through the fronds and past the downed tree trunk. His eyes swept a beach remade by the shelling. Many palm trees were down or leaning precariously. Splinters and scorch marks covered the churned sand.

Bicep counted the helmeted heads popping up from the foxholes. Twenty. He sighed with relief. His troops were fine.

The warships fell silent. Dozens of flat-bottomed landing craft bobbed in the swell, plodding for the island.

"Now it's our turn," Bicep shouted to his troops. "Let's fill them with fear and regret. Weapons ready!"

Each two-person team planted in the sand a black tripod for an M2 machine gun. The .50-caliber M2 had been in use since World War II. It was still frighteningly effective, even on the modern battlefield.

At this moment, Bicep felt a strange connection to World War II soldiers. In 1941, a small American force had tried to defend Wake Island from an overwhelming Japanese assault. History was repeating itself. He hoped for a better outcome this time around.

The Tang landing boats were minutes

from shore. Bicep ran up and down the beach, tapping each of his soldiers on the helmet. "Hold your fire until the ramp drops," he told them. His crews looked tense but ready.

Landing craft approached the V-shaped beach from either side. Bicep returned to his foxhole in the V's center and pushed aside the fallen palm tree. He grabbed his headset and helmet and pulled on a grenade-studded tactical vest. He pressed the headset's talk button.

"The show is about to begin," he said over the I-6 comm net.

The first wave of landing craft sprayed the beach with machine-gun fire. The enemy was trying to goad nervous defenders into revealing their camouflaged positions. Bicep grinned as his gun crews held their fire.

Steel ramps started coming down. Tang soldiers poured from the vessels, splashing into knee-deep water. Bicep's gun crews opened up, sending streams of .50-caliber bullets into the surf. Dozens of Tang soldiers fell. The rest slogged for the beach, leaning forward as if weathering a storm.

Empty landing craft backed away to make room for a second wave. More soldiers stepped into the surf. On the beach, survivors packed into impact craters and crouched behind a sand shelf.

Bicep keyed his headset. "We're ready for some mortar support."

"You got it," Zumi said.

On the airfield, Zumi's three mortar teams began dropping 60-mm rounds down their tubes. They had pre-sighted the beach earlier for accuracy. Bicep watched the first few rounds explode near huddled clusters of Tang soldiers, keeping them pinned to the sand.

"That's effective," he reported to Zumi. "Maintain a steady fire."

Another wave of landing craft released troops and then backed away.

From her control-tower command post, Athena asked for a sitrep, or situation report. Before, Athena could have watched the battle with binoculars. Now, wafting smoke likely blocked her view.

"Enemy troops number about two hundred, with more on the way," Bicep radioed. "We're keeping their heads down for now."

"Tang forces have commenced a secondary landing to the north," Athena replied. "We need to divert some mortar fire in that direction."

Bicep peered northward to Shade's stretch of beach but saw only hazy smoke. "Understood. We'll make do."

At that instant, a Tang hand grenade exploded in front of the nearest American machine-gun nest. The nest's M2 went silent.

Bicep leaped from his foxhole. Both of his soldiers had shrapnel wounds to their arms and shoulders. Medics who had been on standby helped them from the beach.

"Doc, I've got two on the way to you," Bicep said over the comm net as he hopped into the now-empty nest.

"Copy," Doc Dee said. "We'll take good care of them."

CHAPTER 5

CREW OF ONE

Southern Tip of Wake Island
Pacific Ocean
1545 Local / 13 NOV

An M2 gunner usually needed at least one assistant to handle the ammo and watch for threats. In emergencies, an experienced gunner could work alone. Bicep knew the weapon well, and he was determined to get this M2 back in the fight.

He fed a fresh ammo belt into the gun's receiver and pulled back the charging handle. Another wave of landing craft arrived. So many vessels crowded the shallows that they had to jockey for position.

Wait for the ramp to go down, Bicep reminded himself.

A steel ramp lowered directly before him, about a hundred meters away. Bicep pressed the trigger, and the big gun began its earsplitting chatter. Startled soldiers dived from the ramp. Farther back, troops climbed over the boat's side to escape.

Bicep fired in quick bursts to maintain accuracy and keep the weapon from overheating. He punished the landing craft even after its occupants had fled. The vessel's fuel tank exploded, and it partially sank in the shallow water. The burning wreck would make a troublesome obstacle.

Just then, Bicep was knocked backward, the blow tearing his helmet and

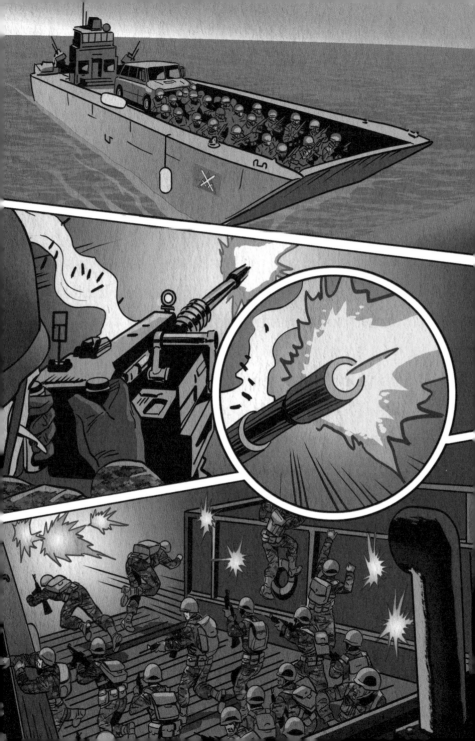

headset from him—another grenade had exploded nearby. He shook his head. His ears were ringing. His lips were wet and salty from a bloody nose.

Strange voices spoke an unfamiliar language. Bicep wondered if he had suffered a concussion.

No, you're okay, he told himself. *Tang soldiers are close*.

He unclipped a grenade from his vest and pulled the pin, then tossed it in the direction of the voices. The grenade detonated. The voices stopped.

Then he pawed around the bottom of the foxhole for his headset. Finding it, he shoved it on and heard Athena's anxious voice. "Bicep, report!"

"I had a close call, but I'm still here."

"You had us worried. What's the sitrep?"

Bicep rose to his knees and scanned the beach. Tang soldiers swarmed like ants. On the water, another wave of landing craft approached.

"We're about to lose the south beach," he said flatly.

"North beach too," Athena replied. "Listen, everyone needs to pull back. We're going to set up a defensive perimeter around the airfield. The mortar crews will lay down a smoke screen to cover your withdrawal."

"Switching to smoke rounds now," Zumi said.

Bicep signaled his gun crews to fall back. Each two-person team would be carrying a hot, heavy machine gun through enemy fire. Bicep's challenge was to do it alone.

Whoomp! Whoomp! Whoomp!

Zumi's smoke rounds began landing. The expanding white clouds merged into a heavy fog that enveloped the beach.

An M2 with a tripod weighed nearly one hundred thirty pounds. Bicep cradled the big gun in his arms, gritting his teeth as hot metal seared his skin. The heavy load slowed his pace across the sand.

The smoke screen dissipated near the airfield, where machine-gun crews settled into new positions. Snipers under Gizmo's leadership crawled on the control tower's roof. Bicep set down the heavy gun.

The beaches were lost. The battle for the airfield would soon begin.

After helping set up claymore mines along the approaches, Bicep climbed the control tower's stairway to the top floor. The room of windows, typically home to air traffic controllers, now served as a combat command center. Officers huddled over maps and spoke into radios. Bicep spotted Athena among them.

"You wanted to see me?" Bicep asked.

Athena pulled him aside and studied him. "First, are you okay?"

Bicep remembered the bloody nose. He touched his sticky lips and cheeks. "I'm fine. Probably looks worse than it is."

"Good. I've got a special mission for you," Athena said in a low voice. "I don't think you'll like it."

"Anything you need."

Athena glanced around the room, confirming no one was listening. When she turned back, her eyes and voice were grave. "A good commander hopes for the best and plans for the worst. We're going to lose the airfield. I need to prepare for that scenario."

Bicep tried to hide his surprise. "Hey, I know it won't be easy, but—"

"We're going to lose," she repeated. "I'll do everything possible to slow them down, but Tang forces outnumber us ten to one. Maybe more."

Bicep shrugged. "Then I'll be sure to get my ten."

"That's the part you won't like. I need you to sit this one out."

He frowned. "What do you mean?"

"Rather than pulling a trigger, you'll be planning our escape."

"Okay." Bicep rubbed his shoulder. She was right—he hated the idea of his friends and fellow soldiers facing the enemy without him.

"It's an important job," Athena said, "and you're the best choice for it."

Bicep straightened and nodded. Athena

always saw the big picture. She wouldn't ask him to do this without a good reason.

Athena led him to a map sprawled across a desk.

"Here we are on Wake Island," she said, pointing at the airfield. "Wake is part of an atoll that has two other islands, Peale and Wilkes. The three islands surround a central lagoon."

"I know," Bicep said. "I put the hovercraft in the lagoon for safety."

"And now I want you to use the hovercraft to establish a fallback position," she said. "If Tang forces do capture the airfield, we'll need a new base."

"Where?"

She tapped a northerly spot on the map. "Peale Island. We'll dig in on Peale."

Bicep studied the mapmaker's

depiction of the island. "Looks like nothing but jungle."

"Desolate, rugged, and wild," Athena agreed. "The perfect stronghold."

"So, we turn Peale into an island fortress. Then what?"

"Then we go on the offensive." Athena's eyes twinkled. "We'll make life miserable for the Tang occupation force."

Bicep grinned. "Will I be able to make up for the fighting I miss?"

She laughed. "I guarantee it."

CHAPTER 6

TACTICAL RETREAT

The Lagoon
Wake Island Atoll
1645 Local / 13 NOV

Tang mortar rounds fell in the shallow water as Bicep fired up the hovercraft's engines. He steered clear of the drop patterns while guiding the vessel for land.

The LCAC hovered on flat ground as easily as it did on water. US soldiers gaped as it came ashore, stirring a mini sandstorm. Bicep's first stop was the base's storehouse. He pulled up in front of the building and lowered his ramp.

Two forklifts trundled aboard with

pallets of supplies. They set down their cargo and returned to the storehouse for more. Another pair of forklifts followed. In minutes, the LCAC received tents, drinking water, food rations, weapons, and equipment.

Meanwhile, Tang infantry pressed their assault on the airfield. Smoke rose from flash points around the perimeter. Small-arms fire crackled like popcorn. Bicep wondered why there was no heavy weaponry, such as tanks and artillery. He suspected the Tang generals did not wish to damage their soon-to-be-acquired airfield. They'd let the infantry fight alone, at the cost of more lives.

"That's everything, sir," called a supply sergeant.

"Did you empty out the weapons lockers?" Bicep yelled back.

The sergeant nodded. "Every last bullet."

Bicep raised the LCAC's ramp and returned to the lagoon. He throttled to full speed, reaching Peale Island in just a few minutes.

As the forklift drivers unloaded pallets onto the beach, Bicep scouted the jungle. It was wild and overgrown, home only to birds and small animals. In the distance, the battle rumbled like thunder.

Once the LCAC had been emptied of supplies, Bicep roared back across the lagoon. His next stop was Doc Dee's aid station, near the front lines. The hovercraft might need to defend itself, so Bicep assigned two forklift drivers to the LCAC's machine guns.

Tang forces now occupied roughly a third of the airfield, including several key buildings. Zumi's mortar crews had fallen back to the lagoon's edge. She pointed him toward Doc Dee's aid station, which had also been forced to move.

The control tower had been evacuated, but vicious fighting still raged around its base. Athena and the command staff worked in an open field, leaning over tables dragged from the cafeteria. Soldiers with rifles tried to protect them as the combat encroached.

Bicep reached the aid station and shut down the LCAC's engines. He had steeled himself for a gruesome scene, but the casualties were light. Medics carried three serious cases aboard on stretchers. The rest of the wounded limped up the ramp on their own. Doc Dee and the medical staff carried surgical equipment.

Tang soldiers had refrained from

firing on the LCAC during the medical evacuation. Once it began picking up combatants, however, the hovercraft became a target. Bicep ducked as a bullet came through the cockpit window, slamming into the back wall. His machine gunners returned fire.

Zumi's mortar teams came aboard. So did Athena and the command staff. Gizmo's snipers climbed the superstructure. They covered Shade's rearguard troops, who kept shooting and hurling grenades toward the enemy until they reached the hovercraft.

"That's everyone," Shade yelled as he came up the ramp. "Get us out of here!"

Bicep revved to full power and turned the hovercraft toward the lagoon. He had scarcely reached water when he saw Tang colors going up the airfield's flagstaff.

A single American had perished in the battle for the airfield—its commander. Captain Molina had taken part in the fierce fighting around the control tower. He'd died instantly when a Tang mortar round landed a few meters away. The new camp on Peale Island was named in his memory.

The I-6 team gathered for an early morning meeting to decide the next move. They stood around a water trailer, filling their canteens as they spoke.

"Our fresh water supply won't last long," Doc Dee warned. "Neither will our rations."

"Spread the word that we need to conserve food and water," Athena said.

"The hovercraft is big enough for everyone," Doc Dee said. "We could be in Hawaii in two days."

Shade shook his head. "Not an option."

"Why not? We can't retake the airfield. A carrier strike group will have to do that."

"True," Shade said. "But until a strike group gets here, we're the only ones who can make a difference."

Zumi frowned. "It doesn't feel like we've made much of a difference so far."

"Right now, the Tang grip on Wake Island is tenuous," Shade said. "In the coming days, they'll dig in like a tick. We need to prevent that."

"Shade's right," Athena said. "The work we do now will save lives when a strike force finally gets here. But there's another reason to stay, one that could upset the balance of power in the Pacific."

Bicep startled as he remembered. "Chalk One."

Athena nodded. "That crumpled

airframe still holds twenty tactical nuclear missiles. It's just a matter of time until Tang troops discover them."

Doc Dee visibly shuddered at the thought of a nuclear-armed Tangonesia. "Forget what I said. We need to stay."

"Agreed," Zumi said. "But how do we keep them away from Chalk One? They own the airfield."

The team mulled over their limited options. Then Gizmo knelt in the sand.

"Check it out," he said. With a twig, he sketched the airfield, then placed a seashell on the long runway. "Chalk One is stranded way out in the open, far from any cover."

He drew an X northwest of the base. "There's a grove of trees here, just past the runway. My snipers and I could infiltrate that grove. We'd be close enough to chase any nosy troops away from Chalk One."

Athena studied the sand diagram. "Perfect. Leave as soon as you're ready."

Gizmo dropped the twig and bolted.

"What other havoc can we cause?" asked Shade.

Bicep picked up the twig and drew a fleet of ships west of the island. "Their invasion fleet still hasn't brought ashore any heavy equipment. The cargo ships must have tanks, artillery, and tons of supplies. We could send a few freighters to the bottom."

Shade wrinkled his brow. "How?"

"Frogman style," Bicep said with a half grin. "The base's storehouse had some scuba gear and underwater explosive packs."

Zumi's eyes widened. "Count me in."

"Me too," said Shade. He turned to Athena. "It's Bicep's specialty, so I'll cede mission authority to him."

"Okay," Athena said. "The three of you can go night swimming. Meanwhile, Doc Dee and I will fortify Camp Molina. The Tang generals probably don't view us as much of a threat right now, but that will change."

"After tonight," Bicep said, "they'll know the fight is far from over."

CHAPTER 7

DEATH SHARK

Wilkes Island
Pacific Ocean
2030 Local / 14 NOV

The frogman operation required stealth, meaning no big, noisy hovercraft. Fortunately, Bicep had found an inflatable rubber dinghy in the LCAC's emergency gear. After dusk, he, Zumi, and Shade carried the dinghy to the waves and began paddling out to sea.

They'd spent the afternoon observing the invasion fleet, which lay a kilometer off the coast of Wilkes Island on the atoll's northwest end. By keeping a log of the fleet's activity, Bicep had been able to figure out which cargo ships to target.

Now, the huge ships loomed like dark buildings. Bicep frowned at the lack of lights. The fleet was following blackout procedures, suggesting its sailors were professional and alert. He had hoped for some smug complacency. The Tang navy, it seemed, would deny him that benefit.

"Let's swim the rest of the way," he said, setting down the paddle. He and the others pulled on their flippers and masks, then made a final oxygen check. Bicep passed out the C-4 explosive packs.

"The timers are synced for seventy minutes from now," he said. "We should be back on the beach by then."

"How do we plant them?" Zumi asked.

"Attach your charges low on the hull in a triangular pattern, spaced about five meters apart," Bicep said. "Hit the arming switch and then come back here."

"What if there's trouble?" Shade asked.

"If anything goes wrong, just swim like crazy for the island. We'll meet on the beach."

The divers slipped into the water and headed off for their respective targets. At six meters deep, Bicep activated his shoulder-mounted spotlight. Its red glow would not reach the surface.

An eerie world surrounded him. He saw strange fish with bulging eyes and slim eels slinking by. Sharks hunted at night, he knew, so he needed to stay vigilant. The ocean—so wild and beautiful—could turn deadly in an instant.

Bicep reached his target. The ship's hull sat low in the water, meaning plenty of cargo was still on board. He kicked to a barnacle-free spot far below the waterline. The explosive packs had a magnetic backing. He held out the first charge. It leaped from his hand and attached to the steel hull with a soft *clang*. He flicked the arming switch. A red dot flashed.

Bicep moved five meters away and repeated the process, then did so once more. When he was finished, three red dots formed the points of a triangle. The charges would explode at the same instant, creating a single, devastating breach. A tremendous surge of seawater would fill the lower decks, leaving the crew no choice but to abandon ship.

He returned to the rubber dinghy and waited. A moment later, Zumi's head popped up from the water.

"That was quite a caper." She grinned.

Shade appeared next. "Did you guys see that coral reef? We need to come back here when—"

"Quiet," Bicep hissed. A motor growled in the distance. He reached for his binoculars. An oddly shaped speedboat was approaching. "I think it's a Protector unmanned surface vehicle. They must be using it for fleet security."

"Dangerous?" Shade asked.

"Its nickname is the Death Shark."

"Yikes," Shade said. "How does it work?"

"A sailor on one of these ships is piloting it remotely with cameras and heat sensors."

Zumi whistled. "What if it spots us?"

"Well," Bicep said, "a Death Shark can carry a machine gun, grenade launcher, or Spike missiles. It depends on the model."

He kept his binoculars trained on the little boat, which held a leisurely course as if on patrol. Then, abruptly, the Death Shark turned and accelerated.

Bicep saw the telltale flicker of a missile launch. "Dive!" he shouted. "Go as deep as you can!"

He leaped headfirst into the water, kicking with all his strength. Seconds later, a white flash came from above. Metal fragments sliced past him like jagged little torpedoes.

Another missile detonated, bringing more shrapnel. Bicep's right arm burned. He kept kicking until he reached the seafloor. The Death Shark passed overhead.

He turned on his spotlight to assess the damage. Blood oozed from pinpricks in the wet suit's left sleeve. His flippers

were shredded. Tiny bubbles streamed from his breathing hose. He worried about Zumi and Shade. Above, the Death Shark made another pass.

Bicep checked his wrist compass and started for the island. The torn flippers gave little help, and the perforated breathing hose sapped his oxygen. His bleeding arm, though a minor injury, had the potential to attract sharks.

Just keep going, he told himself.

After twenty minutes underwater, he rose to the surface. The Tang fleet had come alive. Destroyers circled the cargo ships. Huge spotlights swept the water farther out to sea. Bicep had escaped their search area.

After slipping off the damaged scuba gear, he swam for shore. Soon, gentle waves were nudging him onto the beach.

He stood and walked to the rally point. Zumi and Shade were already there, nursing some cuts and scrapes. The trio exchanged tired smiles and then watched the frantic search.

"Will they check the hulls?" Shade wondered.

"Probably," Bicep said. "I've learned not to underestimate the Tang navy. The big question is if their divers will find the charges in time."

He checked his watch. The muffled underwater explosions would be inaudible from this distance.

The seconds ticked down to zero.

Bicep squinted for any sign of success. The Tang warships continued their manhunt as if nothing had changed. A full minute passed with no observable results.

"They found the charges," Zumi groaned.

"Not necessarily. We just may not be able to—"

A geyser of flame leaped into the night. The blast's heavy report echoed across the open water. Secondary explosions followed. Missiles corkscrewed through the air, and artillery shells climbed skyward. Warships sped away from the deadly fireworks, revealing a stricken vessel that glowed orange like a boiling cauldron.

"We touched off an ammo reserve," Bicep said.

"And look." Shade pointed at two stationary ships. The two freighters were failing to retreat. They merely slumped in the flickering shadows.

"That one is capsizing," Zumi said.

As the big cargo ship rolled over and sank, rescue boats moved in to pluck crewmembers from the water. The second freighter's bow rose high, as if pointing to the stars, and gradually slid below the surface.

Only the burning cargo ship remained. Its fire blazed brightly, giving plenty of light to the rescue operation. At last, it seemed, the sea grew impatient. Flames dimmed as the sinking ship moved lower, until finally darkness returned.

"End of mission," Bicep murmured.

They crossed Wilkes Island and waded into the lagoon.

Bicep sat on a stretcher, marveling at the medical staff's efficiency. The hospital tent looked ready for an influx of patients.

"No offense, Doc, but I hope we put you out of business," he said.

"Fine with me," Doc Dee said without looking up. His tweezers removed another metal shard from Bicep's bicep. "I hope for the best but prepare for the worst."

Athena came in, smiling. "How's he doing, Doc?"

"Nothing a little antiseptic and some skin glue can't fix."

Athena turned to Bicep. "I just got a report from a recon team. They say the Tang's temporary dock is idle. No more offloading of cargo to the airfield."

Bicep nodded. "They'll need a diving bell to get the rest of their supplies."

"Good execution," she said. "Now I've got another mission for you. The recon team spotted Tang units forming on the airfield."

Bicep snorted. "Guess we got their attention."

"They're staying downrange of Gizmo's snipers," Athena said, "but they're definitely massing for a major op. Most likely an assault on Camp Molina, now that they know we're not going to just slink away."

"How can I help?" Bicep asked.

"We're still heavily outnumbered," Athena said. "Maybe we can apply a little psychology. When the Tang soldiers arrive, I'd like to have a surprise ready. Something scary to weaken their resolve."

"A show of force. I can do that."

Athena gripped his shoulder then left.

"Okay," Doc Dee said after removing the last metal sliver and sealing the wound. "Good as new."

"Thanks, Doc," Bicep said absently. He was already lost in thought, planning a spectacular show of force.

The Tang generals faced a tactical dilemma. To attack Peale Island, they first needed to overcome its natural defenses.

An invasion by sea would be difficult due to Peale's high coral reefs. Even the flat-bottomed landing craft would get stuck, leaving Tang soldiers to stumble across sharp coral ledges on their way to the beach.

The generals could try crossing a narrow channel at Wake Island's northern tip. A wooden bridge once connected Wake and Peale Islands, but today only crooked pillars remained. They jutted from the water like old bones. Still, the shallow channel could be waded, but only under heavy fire.

The final option was a beach assault on Peale Island's lagoon-facing side. Here, there were few natural barriers. In fact, the landing craft could fan out across the broad lagoon and deliver their troops all at once. It was the best choice, so Bicep felt no surprise when he saw a line of Tang boats coming across the lagoon late that morning.

"Showtime," he said over I-6's comm net. "They're about twenty minutes out."

"Roger," Athena said. "Go put some fear into them."

He fired up the hovercraft's engines and eased from the beach. Upon reaching the lagoon, he went to full throttle. Two gigantic fans howled, propelling the LCAC forward. It was twice the size of a Tang landing craft and three times as fast.

The LCAC quickly closed the distance, meeting the assault force at the south end of the lagoon. Bicep's machine gunners opened fire, raking the enemy boats. Some Tang soldiers shot back, but most kept their heads down, apparently willing to endure the harassment.

Now it was time for the big surprise. Bicep made a wide turn that placed him behind the Tang boats. As he swept down the formation's rear, his grenadiers went to work. The volunteers hurled dozens of M67 fragmentation grenades.

Most grenades missed the mark, kicking up a harmless spray. The few that did clank onto the deck of a vessel created absolute chaos. One landing craft fell out of formation as its crew desperately tried to put out an engine fire.

The grenade attack spurred Tang troops into action. Shots ricocheted off the hovercraft and peppered its rubber skirt. Bicep noticed a loss of speed and agility. Bullet holes were hindering the skirt's ability to produce lift. He turned for another pass as his machine gunners and grenadiers pressed their attack.

The hovercraft shuddered from a powerful impact. Red lights flashed on the dashboard. Bicep spun in his seat to assess the damage. One of the huge fans had been reduced to twisted metal, likely from a rocket-propelled grenade. He turned the LCAC for Peale Island. It billowed black smoke the entire way.

Bicep made sure all his soldiers disembarked. Then he faced the lagoon once more. The Tang formation was just a few minutes away. Bicep pointed his bow at its center and locked in the heading.

"Thanks for everything," he said, patting the dashboard.

He had a final C-4 explosive pack, which he placed near the high-capacity fuel bladder. He set its timer to sixty seconds and flicked the arming switch. A countdown started. Bicep passed the demolished fan and stood on the stern. He jumped into the neck-deep water.

The LCAC chugged on without him,

trailing black smoke and oily water. A fresh wave of bullets and rocket-propelled grenades ravaged it. The hovercraft listed but stayed on course, arriving at the center of the Tang formation.

The timer reached zero.

A fireball spread across the water, incinerating the LCAC and the nearest Tang boat. Bicep, now standing on the sand, felt a wall of heat rush past. One landing craft swerved to avoid a flaming oil slick. It collided with its neighbor, and both began to sink.

The remaining vessels pushed for shore and dropped their ramps. Hundreds of Tang troops charged onto the beach, their faces twisted in anger. A startled Bicep fell back for the tree line.

The show of force had not frightened the Tang soldiers. It had enraged them.

CHAPTER 9

LAST STAND

Camp Molina Perimeter
Peale Island
1200 Local / 15 NOV

The previous battles had been orderly, textbook engagements. Clearly, the battle for Camp Molina would be different. Revenge-minded Tang soldiers attacked with reckless fury.

The US soldiers, meanwhile, were making their last stand. They had no more fallback positions. The conflict between these two mismatched forces would be decided here and now.

Zumi's mortar teams pounded the

beach. Tang soldiers ignored the bursting shells as they rushed the tree line, quickly overwhelming a string of US outposts. The stunned occupants flew into headlong retreat.

Bicep saw the outpost survivors emerge from the woods, sprinting wildly for the camp. He hopped onto a sandbag wall and waved them inside.

"This way!" he shouted. "Right through this opening. You're safe now."

The soldiers passed through the narrow gap in the camp's perimeter. Bicep then sealed the gap. He jammed the missing wooden spears back into the ground and angled their sharpened tips toward the enemy.

He glanced up and down the sandbagged trench line. Every soldier stared at the woods with rifle or machine gun ready. This time there was no need to yell inspiring words. They were fighting for their lives and they knew it.

Bicep dropped into the waist-high trench and unshouldered his HK416 assault rifle. He rested its foregrip on a sandbag and aimed for the woods.

An anxious silence fell over the camp, like it was inside the eye of a storm.

"Radio check," Athena said on the team's comm net. "Give me a final sitrep."

Zumi replied first. "Mortars ready."

"Snipers ready," Gizmo said.

"Medics ready," Doc Dee said.

"North perimeter ready," Shade said.

Bicep pressed the talk button. "South perimeter ready."

A high sun beat down upon them. Bicep's eyes stung from sweat.

The quiet gave way to a dull roar. It

gradually built into the howl of hundreds of angry voices. The woods twinkled with muzzle flashes. A bullet slammed into a nearby sandbag.

"Wait for targets!" Bicep yelled.

Over the comm net, Shade called for mortars. Bicep heard the familiar *bloop* of rounds leaving their tubes. The mortar barrage began just as Tang forces surged from the woods.

"Now!" Bicep shouted, unleashing a storm of automatic weapons fire.

Enemy soldiers sprinted through the kill zone, seemingly oblivious to the metal blizzard. Bicep had never seen such bitter determination. Dozens fell dead or injured from the withering fire, but still more came. Every casualty appeared to fuel the Tang soldiers' anger.

The first wave of Tang troops swarmed

the perimeter. They pulled down wooden stakes and clambered over sandbags.

"Zumi!" Bicep shouted. "Target my position. Drop your rounds directly on the perimeter."

"What?" Zumi's voice wavered. "I can't."

A Tang soldier leaped into the trench. Bicep raised his rifle stock and struck the man between the eyes. The soldier's knees buckled, and he fell, unconscious, to the ground.

"Hurry!" Bicep yelled. "We're being overrun!"

"Do it, Zumi," Athena ordered.

There was a pause.

"First round in ten seconds," Zumi said grimly.

Bicep climbed onto the sandbag wall and shouted to his soldiers. "Get down! Everyone down now!"

He dived to the trench floor and curled up tight, hands on his ears.

Heavy thuds reverberated in his chest. Sand fell like rain, coating him in a gritty blanket. He imagined the trench walls collapsing, burying him alive.

When Bicep uncovered his ears, the eerie calm had returned. He opened his eyes. The unconscious Tang soldier still lay where he had fallen. Farther down the trench, dazed defenders were getting to their knees and dusting sand from their weapons.

Bicep rose to his feet and surveyed the damage. Tang forces had withdrawn into the woods. Their medics carried wounded soldiers from the battlefield. Stakes and sandbags were scattered everywhere. The desperate tactic had worked, but it had obliterated the perimeter's defenses.

"Report," Athena said.

"We stopped their momentum," Bicep said. "But if they regroup and attack again, we're done."

"All mortar rounds are gone," Zumi reported. "We'll grab our rifles and join you on the trench line."

A new sound broke the silence—the beat of helicopter blades. Bicep's heart leaped. The long-awaited carrier strike group had finally arrived. He pictured an aircraft carrier approaching offshore, surrounded by cruisers and destroyers and dispatching Seahawk helicopters for a last-minute rescue.

Then the choppers appeared, and Bicep's heart plunged to new depths. They were Tang helicopters, including the pair of Hind armored gunships. This was the commando squadron that had appeared over Wake Island on the first morning of the invasion.

"They saved their commandos for the final blow," Shade noted somberly.

From the woods, shouting began once more. The infantry soldiers no doubt planned to help wipe out the Americans.

"Does anyone have any ideas?" Athena asked.

The I-6 comm net went quiet. They were out of options.

The Hind gunships opened fire, striking the camp with their autocannons. The other choppers held a low hover as commandos descended on thick ropes.

Tang infantry emerged from the woods. Bicep looked down the sight of his HK416 but found it difficult to line up a target. He was hyperventilating.

Stay calm, he told himself.

After a few seconds of controlled breathing, Bicep tried again. He squeezed the trigger, and a Tang soldier tumbled to the ground.

A shadow swept past. An armored gunship was moving in to strike the trench line. The black barrel of its autocannon swung directly at him.

This time, Bicep didn't feel scared. His breath came easily. He raised his rifle, determined to go out fighting.

The gunship suddenly vanished in a fiery sphere of orange, blue, and yellow. Bicep watched in shock as spinning blades and flaming debris drifted earthward.

An F/A-18E Super Hornet streaked overhead, no more than one hundred fifty meters from the ground. The pilot waggled his wings before passing from view. Bicep pumped his fist and joined the outburst of cheers. The strike force had arrived after all.

More Super Hornets zoomed over the island. An air-to-air missile found the second Tang gunship, creating another huge fireball. The remaining Tang helicopters broke from their hover. Dangling commandos clung to the ropes as the choppers fled at top speed.

A flight of Seahawks appeared, just as Bicep had imagined, but not for a rescue. Each one touched down long enough to deposit a squad of marines, who immediately joined the fight.

"Let's go," Bicep shouted, leading the combined force forward. "Pour it on!"

Stubborn Tang soldiers tried to hold their ground, but only briefly. Momentum had turned against them.

The invasion was over.

Tang soldiers scrambled through the woods and down the beach, then piled aboard their landing craft. The vessels chugged across the lagoon, eager to reach open sea and their fleet.

Bicep stood on the beach watching them go. Moments earlier, he had faced a near-certain end. There was still the airfield to reclaim and the Tang fleet to subdue. But the tide of battle had shifted so suddenly, so profoundly, it felt like a dream.

Doc Dee approached and stood beside him. "You okay?"

"How did we get so lucky?" Bicep asked.

Doc Dee patted him on the back. "I suppose you could say we made our own luck. We never gave up."

Southern Tip of Wake Island
Pacific Ocean
1330 Local / 17 DEC

The three-day battle had claimed
fourteen American lives and left thirty
injured. Tang losses were thought to
be at least tenfold. After reclaiming the
airfield, Carrier Strike Group Five had
chased the invasion fleet all the way back
to Tangonesia. At the United Nations,
a sheepish Tang diplomat had issued
a formal apology and agreed to pay
reparations.

The I-6 team had returned to Pearl
Harbor for debriefing. One month later,
they were back on Wake Island as guests

of the new commander. To Bicep's delight, this visit included plenty of good food and relaxing beach time.

Most of the island's battle scars were already gone. The foxholes had been filled in. Damaged buildings looked new again. Chalk One had been hauled from the runway. Its nuclear cargo was secure.

Bicep was playing beach volleyball when his foot touched a warm piece of metal. He reached into the sand and found a .50-caliber shell casing. As he rolled the empty brass cylinder in his hand, he realized he was standing on the spot of his machine-gun nest. Even after all this time, it still felt like a dream.

"Get cleaned up, people," Athena called from the tree line. "Ceremony is in thirty minutes."

Bicep returned to his room, showered,

and put on his dress blues. He walked with his teammates to the Wake Island Defenders Memorial, which had been erected after World War II to honor those who had fought here.

A hushed crowd waited to see the monument's new addition. The throng of dignitaries and reporters edged forward as the sculpture was unveiled. I-6 stood at attention in the back with the honor guard. Flags snapped in the breeze. Passing seagulls cawed.

When the speeches were done and the crowd had left for a banquet, I-6 approached the sculpture for a closer look. It was a sea turtle with details of the battle etched into its shell, including the names of those killed in action.

"It's beautiful, but I don't get it," Bicep said. "Why a sea turtle?"

"They can live a hundred years, so many cultures associate sea turtles with survival and perseverance," Doc Dee explained.

"That's not all," Shade said. "Just one in a thousand hatchlings makes it to adulthood, so an adult sea turtle is extremely lucky. It beat the odds."

Bicep nodded thoughtfully. "Luck and perseverance. That's how we survived too."

"And look at this," Athena said, kneeling beside the sculpture.

The team gathered around her and exchanged broad smiles. A special symbol adorned the turtle's head—a number six with parts marked out of it.

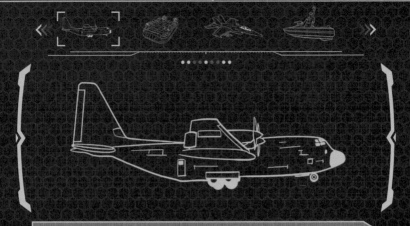

WC-130J Weatherbird

This aircraft is used for weather data collection. It flies into storms to track information on the storms' movement, size, and power. Five crewmembers work on each mission.

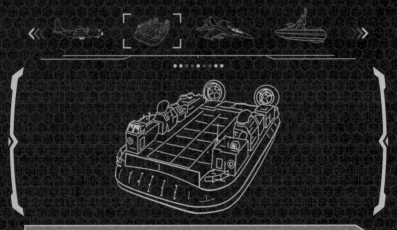

Landing Craft, Air Cushion (LCAC)

This hovercraft can move at high speeds on land or sea. It can carry up to 75 tons (68 metric tons) of cargo and personnel from ship to shore.

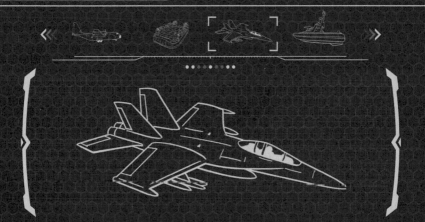

F/A-18E Super Hornet

This single-seat aircraft flies from aircraft carriers and is used by the US Navy for air strikes with precision weapons.

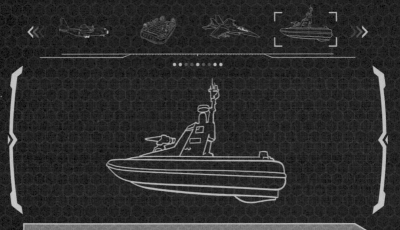

Protector Unmanned Surface Vehicle (USV)

This remote-controlled sea vehicle has infrared sensors and cameras for tracking, as well as precision weaponry for targeted strikes.

GEAR SPOTLIGHT

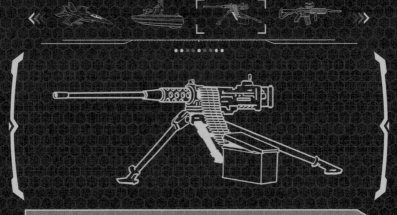

M2 Machine Gun

First developed for World War II, the M2 automatic weapon is still used today. It fires heavy rounds with accuracy across long distances.

HK416 Assault Rifle

This gun is a gas-operated automatic weapon that has an effective range of approximately 1,600 feet (500 m). It can be safely fired underwater.